POLAR MELTDOWN

J. BURCHETT & S. VOGLER

STONE ARCH BOOKS
a capstone imprint

Wild Rescue books are published by Stone Arch Books
A Capstone Imprint
1710 Roe Crest Drive,
North Mankato, Minnesota 56003
www.capstonepub.com

First published by Stripes Publishing Ltd.
1 The Coda Centre
189 Munster Road
London SW6 6AW
© Jan Burchett and Sara Vogler, 2012
Interior art © Diane Le Feyer of Cartoon Saloon, 2012

Library of Congress Cataloging-in-Publication Data
Burchett, Jan.
Polar meltdown / written by Jan Burchett [and] Sara Vogler ; illustrated by Diane Le Feyer ; cover illustration by Sam Kennedy.
p. cm. -- (Wild rescue)
Originally published: London : Stripes, 2009.
ISBN 978-1-4342-3769-9 (library binding)
1. Twins--Juvenile fiction. 2. Brothers and sisters--Juvenile fiction. 3. Polar bear--Alaska--Juvenile fiction. 4. Wildlife conservation--Alaska--Juvenile fiction. 5. Alaska--Juvenile fiction. 6. Adventure stories. [1. Twins--Fiction. 2. Brothers and sisters--Fiction. 3. Polar bear--Fiction. 4. Bears--Fiction. 5. Wildlife conservation--Fiction. 6. Alaska--Fiction. 7. Adventure and adventurers--Fiction.] I. Vogler, Sara. II. Le Feyer, Diane, ill. III. Kennedy, Sam, 1971- ill. IV. Title.
PZ7.B915966Po 2012
823.914--dc23   2011025563

Cover Art: Sam Kennedy
Graphic Designer: Russell Griesmer
Production Specialist: Michelle Biedscheid

Design Credits: Shutterstock 51686107 (p. 4-5),
Shutterstock 51614464 (p. 148-149, 150, 152)

Printed in the United States of America in Stevens Point, Wisconsin.
072012
006878R

TABLE OF CONTENTS

CHAPTER 1: POLAR PROBLEMS...............7

CHAPTER 2: GEARING UP..................16

CHAPTER 3: THE HERITAGE CENTER........27

CHAPTER 4: LUCKY LUKIE................47

CHAPTER 5: TROUBLED WATERS............63

CHAPTER 6: WHITEOUT...................73

CHAPTER 7: SHELTER....................85

CHAPTER 8: STRANGE LIGHTS............94

CHAPTER 9: SLURPY AND POKEY.........110

CHAPTER 10: WILD RIDE................122

CHAPTER 11: RAT RACE.................131

CHAPTER 12: SAFE AND SOUND...........138

TARGET:

POLAR BEAR CUBS

MISSION

BEN WOODWARD
WILD Operative

ZOE WOODWARD
WILD Operative

WILD RESCUE

BRIEFING

WILDRESCUE

Animal print
identification — 49 out of 50
Congratulations, Wild Operative
Zoe Woodward!

CHAPTER 1

POLAR PROBLEMS

Zoe hit ENTER on the keyboard in front of her. "I finished before you did!" Zoe bragged to her twin brother, Ben. Zoe's test score flashed up on the screen. She read it aloud. "Animal print identification — 49 out of 50. Congratulations, WILD operative Zoe Woodward!"

Ben finished his test a few seconds after Zoe. "You may have finished first," he said, pointing at his screen, "but I got all fifty questions correct."

Ben glanced at Zoe's results. "So you couldn't tell which print was from a moose's hoof?" he asked.

"That was a difficult question," Zoe said. "All the prints looked the same, so I had to guess."

Ben grinned. "So did I," he said. Ben pushed his chair back and looked around at the WILD Education Center's row of computer terminals. Next to them was a huge reference area filled with books and manuals, maps, and charts. "This place is so cool," he said. "In fact, everything we've done here at WILD HQ has been awesome. The climbing wall was the best."

"Canoeing was my favorite," said Zoe.

Ben and Zoe weren't normal teenagers. They were the youngest operatives in WILD, a top-secret environmental organization.

The head of the organization was their uncle, Dr. Stephen Fisher. He had invited them to spend summer vacation at WILD. The headquarters were hidden deep underground in a remote island. Lately, they'd been doing a series of exercises to improve their physical and mental skills for future WILD missions. They did endurance challenges, tracking practices, and several brain-bending puzzles and tests.

"I'll be sad when we have to go back home," Zoe said.

"It's pretty awesome here," agreed Ben. "I wish we could stay longer."

Just then, the door slid open. The lanky figure of Uncle Stephen appeared. He was wearing a white lab coat, a straw hat, and brightly striped shorts. Zoe tried not to giggle at his weird outfit.

"Good job, Ben and Zoe," their uncle said. "You've passed all your challenges with flying colors so far. There's just one last little test."

Ben and Zoe shot each other curious glances. Their uncle smiled, then tossed them a glass eye.

Ben snatched it out of the air before Zoe could grab it. They both knew what the eye meant. They weren't going home after all because Uncle Stephen had a new rescue mission for them!

They stared at the eyeball. The glass eyes were always little clues about a specific animal that was endangered.

"It's dark," said Ben. "The pupil is huge."

"Looks like a teddy bear's eye," Zoe said.

Uncle Stephen grinned. "You're getting close, Zoe," he said.

"The most endangered bear I can think of is the polar bear," said Ben.

"Exactly!" their uncle said. "And I've got a pair of bears in the Arctic that need your help. Come with me to the WILD Control Room."

Ben and Zoe eagerly followed him along the hallway to the Control Room's ID reader. They both placed their fingertips on the electronic pad.

"Print identification complete," said an electronic voice.

The door opened to reveal the center of WILD HQ. It was a brightly lit room filled with operatives, all of them seated in front of busy computer screens.

Uncle Stephen went over to a computer and opened a website. "This was posted on a blog today," he said. "It's from a veterinarian named Theo Airut. He lives in an Inupiat community in Fairwood, Alaska. I often read Theo's blog entries because he seems like a good man who cares for the animals in Alaska. It also keeps me up to date with current events out there."

Uncle Stephen pointed at the top of the webpage. "Erika has set the computer to alert us to any problems posted on the blog," he said. "And this entry certainly made the alarm bells ring."

"A local man brought the body of a polar bear into the village today," Zoe read aloud. "How sad!"

Ben scrolled down the entry. "He had gone on a fishing expedition and a bear attacked him," Ben read. "He had to shoot it to save his own life. Then he brought the body back for its fur."

"Theo asked to see the bear's body," Uncle Stephen said. "He's posted several recent entries about the bears not getting enough to eat, so he wanted to check this bear's health. It's very unusual for a polar bear to attack a human, but this one was starving."

Uncle Stephen looked grim. "I'm afraid global warming is taking its toll on their numbers. I'm sure you've heard all about the polar ice cap shrinking."

Ben and Zoe nodded sadly. They knew all about the threats of global warming.

Uncle Stephen frowned. "Seals normally build their homes in the thick ice shelves," he said. "But because the ice has been thinner these last few years, the seals aren't having as many cubs."

"And seals are the main source of food for polar bears," added Zoe.

Uncle Stephen nodded. "Exactly," he said. "The seals have a lot of body fat. By eating the seals, the bears develop important layers of body fat that keep them warm and allow them to go without food for long periods of time."

"If this bear's already dead, then what's our mission?" Ben asked, puzzled.

"The vet's examination showed something very troubling," Uncle Stephen said. "The dead bear had recently given birth."

"That's awful!" cried Zoe. "It means there are motherless cubs out there alone in the wild."

Stephen nodded grimly. "The Arctic is a very hostile terrain," he said. "This mission will be your most difficult one yet. You need to find those cubs before it's too late."

CHAPTER 2

GEARING UP

Ben and Zoe could barely contain their excitement. This mission would be like nothing they'd ever done before. "Any clues to where we should start looking?" Zoe asked her uncle.

"The blogger didn't say where the bear attacked," said Uncle Stephen. "You'll have to figure that out when you get there."

"The mother wouldn't have strayed far from her cubs," Ben said. "Polar bears build birthing dens."

"And they make their dens in the snow," Zoe said, "and stay in them for months at a time."

"That's right," said Uncle Stephen, nodding.

"We need to find out where the attack took place," said Zoe, "and start our search there."

"That's a good plan," said Uncle Stephen. "Most bears give birth in December and January. When the cubs are about two or three months old, they mother starts bringing them out into the open. That means our little orphan cubs could have started exploring already, but they'll still be dependent on their mother for milk."

The door opened. A smiling young woman named Erika Bohn walked in. She was Uncle Stephen's second in command.

"I just received the latest weather reports for Fairwood," Erika said. "It's five degrees below zero — not including the wind chill. And it's snowing heavily."

Zoe gasped. "That's really cold," she said. "And won't it be mostly dark this time of year?"

"In the middle of winter, yes," Uncle Stephen said. "But since it's March, there will be about twelve hours of daylight."

Erika tapped a screen and brought up a map of the Arctic Circle near the coast of Alaska. "Here's Fairwood," she said. "That's the village where the fisherman lives. I'll take you there so you can find out more information from him. Curious questions from a couple of kids won't look suspicious. I'll pretend to be your mother and we'll say we're tourists."

Uncle Stephen nodded. "Then you two will head out on your own to search for the bear cubs while Erika travels farther along the coast," he added.

Erika pointed at the display map north of Fairwood. "There's a new oil-drilling project near Fairwood," she said. "We're worried that pollution from the drilling will add to the problems that global warming is already causing for the animals nearby. I'm going there to investigate."

Uncle Stephen pulled out a small crate from underneath a workstation and rummaged around inside. "You'll need my latest invention, of course," said "I'm very excited about the RAT!"

With a flourish, their uncle pulled out two streamlined snowboards with miniature engines at the rears.

The devices were about half the size of normal snowboards and could fold in half for easier travel. Zoe and Ben's eyes were wide. They had never seen anything like them.

"The RAT," Uncle Stephen explained, "is also know as the Rapid Arctic Traveler. I've made them from a special material I've developed. They're so strong that an elephant could use them — if it could fit its feet into the footholds. And they're made entirely from recycled materials."

Uncle Stephen placed one of the RATs on the ground and stood on it. He kicked the engine into life with his heel. The RAT wobbled dangerously beneath Uncle Stephen's feet.

"Dr. Fisher!" said Erika. "Remember what happened last time you tried to use it."

"I thought I'd be safe in the hallway," Uncle Stephen said. "How was I supposed to know that James was about to come out of the cafeteria with a bowl of ice cream?"

Ben laughed. "I wish I'd seen that!" he said.

"I looked like a milkshake afterward," Uncle Stephen said. He reluctantly stepped off the RAT.

"It's just like skateboarding," said Erika. "And I know you two are experts at that. The RAT glides across the snow. It's very flexible and can handle even the bumpiest ground. The engine runs on solar-powered batteries, and it can run for forty-eight hours without a charge."

"Cool!" Zoe said. "I can't wait to try it out." She picked up one of the RATs. "It's really light."

"And now for the rest of your equipment," said Erika. "You'll need your BUGs and warm clothing." She opened a drawer and handed Zoe and Ben two small devices. The BUGs looked like handheld video game consoles, but they were really complex machines that performed a wide range of things like satellite mapping and animal tracking.

"I really wish you'd let us hold on to these between missions," Ben said, scrolling through the menu.

Uncle Stephen chuckled. "Don't forget to pack your thermal wear," he said. "It'll be as vital as your BUGs on this mission."

Erika led Ben and Zoe over to the WILD stockroom. It looked like the inside of a cave, but it was filled with amazing technological devices, clothes for all possible climates, and countless half-finished inventions that Uncle Stephen was still working on.

Erika pulled two backpacks off the shelf. "I've already put a tent in one of these," she said, "as well as your ultra-light thermal sleeping bags." Then she took two baby bottles and some powdered milk from a cabinet and stuffed them inside.

"These packets are specially formulated to match the rich milk of a polar bear mother," Erika explained. She pointed at a box near Zoe. "Grab those for me, will you, Zoe?" she asked.

Zoe bent down and pulled two furry fleeces out of the box. "What are these?" she asked.

"Slings," said Uncle Stephen, appearing in the doorway. "The cubs will be about the size of large cats by now. When you find them, you'll need something to carry them. The fur will make them think you're their mother — we don't want them to get used to being around humans."

Zoe and Ben stashed the slings in their backpacks. Erika made two piles of clothes for them to take, and then she showed them the special side pockets that kept the folded RATs hidden and warm.

Uncle Stephen chuckled. "Looks like Erika's having you pack everything but the kitchen sink!" he said. "She's right, though. You have to be prepared for the worst out there."

Erika grinned at Uncle Stephen. She picked up two pairs of goggles and handed them to Ben and Zoe. "These are specially designed for the Arctic," she said. "They act as snow goggles, but when you press the logo here they become thermogoggles."

Erika touched the small symbol on one side of the device in Ben's hand. Immediately, the lower half of the glass darkened.

Erika handed the goggles to Ben and Zoe. "Awesome!" said Ben.

The twins heaved their backpacks onto their shoulders and held their Arctic clothing over their arms.

"We're ready!" Zoe said. Ben nodded.

"Good luck," said Uncle Stephen. "While you're searching, I'll start looking for somewhere that takes polar bear orphans."

Ben turned to face Zoe. "Well, what are we waiting for?" he asked. "We've got cubs to save!"

CHAPTER 3

THE HERITAGE CENTER

Erika landed the airplane at the little airport in Fairwood, Alaska. It was a bright morning and the sun glinted on the snow.

"The flight only took seven hours!" said Ben. "This plane must be super fast."

Erika smiled as she took off the pilot's headset. "Yes, your uncle's very pleased with his new plane design," she said. "It's all made from recycled products and looks just like an ordinary private jet. You're the first passengers to travel in it."

Zoe wrinkled her nose. "I see he's still using chicken poo for his special fuel," she said. All WILD vehicles ran on eco-friendly — and smelly — fuels.

"It doesn't quite smell the same," Ben said. "There's a new smell, too."

"Good nose," said Erika. "Stephen recently put egg yolks in the mixture. That makes for a much more efficient fuel."

Zoe's eyes went wide. "Weird," she said, "but pretty cool, too."

Zoe and Ben picked up their bulging backpacks. "Hats, gloves, and everything else on before I open the door," said Erika. "And don't take anything off while you're outside. Frostbite can occur after just minutes of exposure."

Ben and Zoe were already wearing warm windbreakers and long underwear.

They both zipped themselves into white padded waterproof pants and jackets, then pulled on their masks and gloves.

Ben grinned. "Warm as toast!" he said.

They all stepped down on to the tarmac. Their breaths made clouds in the freezing air.

Zoe looked around the desolate airstrip. There was a single building that rose up from the flat snow all around. "It's so cold!" she said. "The air's freezing the inside of my nose!" She tried not to think about the poor cubs huddled in their den.

"Follow me," Erika said, briskly heading toward the airport offices. "Once we're through passport control, our taxi will be arriving to take us to the Inupiat Heritage Center. It's a good starting place to find the information we need."

Erika, Ben, and Zoe were soon waiting outside the airport. In the distance across the white landscape they could see a group of houses. They seemed to extend a long way down the shore.

Ben peered down a snow-covered road marked by a row of telephone poles. "I think I see our taxi," he said, "and it looks pretty awesome!"

Zoe followed his gaze. She gasped when she saw a large sled gliding toward them, pulled by a team of happy huskies. The sled pulled up next to Ben and Zoe.

The huskies panted heavily as a stocky man dressed in fur-trimmed animal skin jumped off the sled. "Ms. Bohn?" he said with a broad smile.

Erika smiled and nodded. "Pleased to meet you," she said. "These are my children, Ben and Zoe."

"Welcome to Alaska," the man said. "My name's Charlie."

Ben and Zoe admired the sled. "This is going to be great!" Zoe exclaimed. "Can we get in, Mom?"

The twins gave each other a secret grin. They were used to Erika taking on different roles for their missions, but it was still funny to pretend she was their mother.

"Of course, dear," Erika said with a slight grin. "But no pushing or shoving."

The children scrambled aboard. They settled themselves on the long bench, and covered their legs with a blanket.

Zoe kept her eye on the dogs. One of them looked younger and fluffier than the others. It was rolling in the snow and barking excitedly.

"How sweet!" Zoe said. "I just want to hug it."

Ben groaned. "Zoe's experiencing cuteness overload again," he said.

"Leave your sister alone," Erika said. She rolled her eyes at Charlie.

The twins watched Charlie say a few sharp words to the dog. "That one's just finished her training," he told them. He climbed onto the sled. "She'll be a great sled dog when she grows up."

The huskies were already tensing their muscles, anxious to get moving again. Charlie urged the huskies forward with some words in a language they didn't understand. The sled began to glide over the snow in a wide arc. Then it settled into its previous tracks and quickly picked up speed.

As they raced along, Ben and Zoe saw that the landscape was very flat. The snow was deep and undisturbed, except for a single bare tree that was poking up through the snow.

In spite of his warm clothes, Ben shivered. The cold was like nothing he'd experienced before.

"Do you go everywhere on dog sleds?" Zoe asked the driver.

Charlie grinned at Zoe. "Only when I'm transporting tourists," he said. "We know tourists like to see the old way of life of the Inupiat people, which is also why I dress in the traditional Inupiat furs. Normally we use motorized sleds."

"Cool!" exclaimed Ben. "But what do the dogs do, then?"

"There are enough tourists to keep them busy," Charlie said, chuckling. As the sledge turned, a sparkling expanse of ice came into view, broken by small channels of dark water. "The Arctic Ocean," Charlie announced.

"It looks so beautiful!" Zoe said.

"And cold," Ben added.

Charlie nodded. "The temperature of the water is nearly freezing this time of year."

Charlie nodded at Zoe and Ben. "Take care to not get wet out here," he said. "Hypothermia can occur after mere minutes of exposure." Ben shot Zoe a concerned look.

The sled joined a wider road. Eventually, they came to a short main street of tourist shops and family restaurants. Other roads branched away, lined with single-story houses painted in bright colors.

Once they reached the far end of the street, the driver urged the dogs through a gateway. They stopped outside a large brick building with a gently sloping, snow-covered roof. It stood right next to the shore of the ocean.

A row of flags flapped in the wind. Ben recognized the deep blue of the Alaskan flag with its yellow stars.

Ben jerked his thumb toward the flag. "That's the North Star," he said. He pointed at the largest star. "And that's the Plough constellation — also known as the big Dipper or the Great Bear."

"Thanks for the lecture, showoff," Zoe said, chuckling. She leaned in close to Ben and added, in a whisper, "But the Great Bear's just right for our mission." Ben nodded and smiled.

They jumped out of the sled. Erika paid Charlie. The children gazed in awe at a huge skull that was displayed outside the Heritage Center.

"Look at that!" Ben said. "It's as big as a car!"

"That's from a bowhead whale," said Charlie. "You'll learn all about the history of whaling inside."

Iñupiat Heritage Center

Although she tried to hide it, Ben saw a look of disapproval on Zoe's face. "I bet that was hunted," she said under her breath.

"We have to accept that it's their way of life," Ben muttered to her. "The Inupiat rely on whale hunting for food and income."

"I know," Zoe said. "It's just so cruel."

Ben turned to face Charlie. "We were hoping to meet the fisherman who got attacked by a polar bear," he said. "Do you know where we can find him?"

"Lukie's getting famous!" said Charlie. "You might find him inside. He looks after our whaling display when he's not fishing."

They thanked him and pushed open the swinging doors to the Heritage Center. Pleasant, warm air hit them immediately. They left their coats, masks, and backpacks in the coatroom and glanced around at their surroundings.

The center was a huge, open building with cabinets full of Inupiat traditional clothing and cooking utensils. Beautifully crafted harpoons hung from the ceiling.

Zoe walked over to look at the photographs of whaling expeditions that were stretched along one long wall. Meanwhile, Ben went right for the café in the corner and began to browse through the menu.

"You can't be hungry already," Zoe said, rolling her eyes. "You finished two sandwiches and a whole pizza on the plane!"

"That was hours ago!" Ben said. "I'm starving."

"We have to find the fisherman first," Zoe insisted. Ben frowned, but he followed Zoe away from the café.

A woman was stacking postcards into slots on a stand. Zoe walked up to her and tapped her lightly on the shoulder.

"Excuse me," Zoe said. "We heard about a man who got attacked by a polar bear. We'd like to hear his story. Is he here today?"

The woman put down the postcards. "You must mean Lukie," she said. "That young man's always taking risks. Now everyone's talking about his brush with death. I haven't seen him this morning."

"What about Theo Airut?" asked Zoe. "It was his blog that told us all about the attack. Perhaps we could speak to him instead?"

The woman looked surprised at Zoe's persistence. "We're doing a school project on polar bears," Ben said quickly.

"That's why you're so interested," the woman said. "There are plenty of people here who have seen polar bears, but most of us keep our distance!" She nodded at Erika, now standing behind them. "It's nice to see kids so interested in their schoolwork. You must be proud of them."

"I am," said Erika. "They never let me down."

"Aw, Mom," protested Ben. "You're so embarrassing."

"Do you know where Lukie was when the attack happened?" Zoe asked the woman.

"We want to draw a map for our project and mark the exact spot of the attack," added Ben. "It'll make it more exciting to read."

"I wish I could help," said the woman, "but I don't know."

"Would Mr. Airut know?" asked Zoe.

"He's not here," said the saleswoman. "He's gone to Anchorage for a few days for a conference." She smiled. "We're a small community, so we all know each other's business."

The saleswoman saw Ben and Zoe's disappointed faces. "Are you sticking around?" she asked. Ben and Zoe nodded. "Lukie should be back later."

They thanked her and walked away. "What do we do now?" Ben asked Zoe.

"Time to eat," said Erika. Ben rubbed his hands together eagerly at the thought of dinner. "I'm going to find somewhere quiet to contact Stephen for an update on the oil drilling project," Erika added in a low voice. "Will you be all right on your own, children?" she said louder, as the saleswoman walked by.

"Give us a break, Mom," Ben said, pretending to be annoyed by the question.

Erika headed off for the coat room. "Try to behave yourselves," she said.

After eating a plate of fried fish and a giant chocolate chip muffin, Ben and Zoe walked around the displays of whaling memorabilia.

Zoe and Ben pretended to be very interested in the exhibits, but they glanced around carefully whenever someone new came into the center. Not a single one of them ended up being Lukie.

"Time's running out," Zoe said anxiously. "Those cubs aren't going to survive long without their mother."

CHAPTER 4

LUCKY LUKIE

"We're not giving up," said Ben. "See that sign by the door? They're building igloos and boats outside. Someone else might know Lukie's story and have the information we need."

Zoe and Ben pulled on their coats, gloves, and masks. They pushed open the swinging door and stepped into the bitter cold. A freezing wind blew by, making the flags flap violently. They could hear the ice cracking against the shore as the waves washed in.

Zoe stared at a display board that showed maps of the Arctic and the changes that had occurred over the years. "Look at this," she said. "Thirty years ago, there was about three times as much old ice as there is now."

"What's old ice?" asked Ben.

"Old ice is the permanent Arctic ice cap," said Zoe. "And according to this, it's getting smaller very quickly." She read aloud, "'Each year, old ice is replaced with newer, thinner ice that melts more easily in the summer.'"

"That's bad news for the polar bears," said Ben. "There will be even fewer seals for them to eat."

They walked through an arch made of whale rib bones. Zoe followed Ben down a cleared path toward a circle of snow bricks.

An old man in traditional clothes was squatting by the circle, cutting bricks out of the ice with a long knife. His thick black hair stuck out from under his hood.

"Cool!" exclaimed Ben. "I didn't know people made igloos anymore."

The man looked up and nodded as Ben and Zoe approached. "Not many of us learn how to build them these days," he said. "Eskimos like me used to build igloos when they traveled many miles over the ice to hunt."

"Eskimos?" Zoe repeated. "I thought we weren't supposed to call you by that name."

The old man's wrinkled face grinned. "You've heard it's an insult to our people?" he asked. "It's not used in Canada, but here in Alaska we are proud to call ourselves Inupiat Eskimos. But you can call me by my name, Amaguq."

"How long does it take to build an igloo, Amaguq?" Ben asked. "I've always wanted to make one."

"We don't have time to chat," Zoe whispered to Ben. But Amaguq was obviously pleased to talk about his craft.

"For a skilled worker like me, a few hours," Amaguq said. He cut a new block and trimmed it so that it fit perfectly into the igloo wall. "An igloo makes a perfect shelter for hunters who were away for weeks at a time on the ice." He put his knife down. "Of course, if they needed shelter in a hurry they'd just dig a snow hole in a bank."

"Are they easier to build?" asked Ben.

"Much easier," Amaguq said. "You just dig a hole, keeping the entrance away from the wind if at all possible. Most importantly, you must not forget to make an air hole."

"That's interesting," Ben said as the old man finished speaking.

"I think so, too," Zoe said. "Maybe we can put it in our project. We're studying this area — maybe you can help us. We'd like to write about Lukie, the fisherman who works here. He's the one who was attacked by the polar bear."

"You'd have to ask Lukie that," Amaguq said.

"We'd love to talk to him," said Zoe. "But he's not around at the moment."

"I'm sure he'll get here soon," Amaguq said. "He promised me he would repair one of the old canoes in the whaling display."

"So he's not out fishing?" asked Ben.

Amaguq picked up his knife and began to cut another snow brick. "Not today," he said. "There's going to be a snowstorm later."

The children thanked him and retraced their steps toward the Heritage Center. "Glad the weather's stopped Lukie from going fishing," said Ben. "Now we'll get to talk to him sooner.

Zoe frowned. "True," she said, "but there's one thing you're forgetting — we're the ones who might get caught in the snowstorm now."

"We'll be all right," Ben said. He smiled cheerfully. "We've got our tent, remember?"

They reached the door to the center. "I hope Lukie's arrived," said Ben.

"I hope he doesn't think it's strange that we want to know where he was attacked," Zoe said. "We have to be careful what we ask, remember?"

Ben grinned. "Actually I was planning to say, 'Hi, we work for WILD, which is a top secret organization that we can't tell you about, and we're on an undercover mission.'"

Zoe pushed him into a pile of soft snow. Then she scooted off, giggling, to avoid a volley of snowballs from her brother. She almost collided with a young man in a bright red snow jacket who was making his way down the path.

"Hi there, kid," he said, a big smile on his face. Just then, one of Ben's snowballs hit him in the chest.

Ben ran up to them with an embarrassed look on his face. "I'm so sorry!" he said as the young man brushed the snow off his jacket. "I was aiming at my sister."

The man grinned. "No problem!" he said. "I heard there were two kids out here who wanted to know about my encounter with the bear. I guess I've found you — or I guess you've found me! Lukie's the name."

"I'm Zoe, and this is Ben," said Zoe. "We read about you on Mr. Airut's blog before we came away on holiday. We'd be very interested to hear about your encounter with the polar bear."

"If I had a dollar for every time I've been asked to tell this story, I'd be a rich man," said Lukie, his eyes twinkling. "I could give you a tale of great bravery. I could tell you how I tracked down the mighty snow beast and slayed it with my bare hands. But in truth, I was just lucky."

"What happened?" asked Ben.

"I was out ice fishing," Lukie said, "and she suddenly appeared less than fifteen feet away. I knew I had to let her get my scent so that she could identify me as human. Polar bears usually back away from humans."

"But she didn't," said Zoe.

"No. She just kept staring hard at me with her deep, dark eyes," Lukie said. "And the entire time, she was baring her teeth and hissing at me."

"That sounds like one angry bear," Ben said.

"That's for sure," Lukie said. "I stood as tall as I could and waved my arms to scare her, but it didn't work."

Lukie raised his arms over his head. "But then she began to move toward me!" he said. "The next thing I knew, she was lowering her head and charging right at me!"

He roared, making Ben and Zoe jump back. They grinned at each other, a little embarrassed. "I had to think quickly," he said. "I knew I'd never outrun her, so there was only one thing I could do. I fumbled for my gun and somehow managed to get one shot off just before she reached me."

"The blog we read said she had recently given birth," said Zoe. "Wasn't that unusual? I mean, for a mother to leave her cubs?"

Lukie thought for a moment. "I guess so," he said. "I remember Theo said she was very thin. She must have been starving."

"So she thought you were a meal?" Ben asked.

Lukie nodded. "I was sorry to kill her," he said, "but it was either her or me."

"Did you see any cubs?" Zoe asked.

"I can see you're an animal lover, Zoe," Lukie said. "I saw no sign of any cubs. I didn't know then that she was a mother, and I didn't stick around in case there were any more hostile bears around. I couldn't just leave the carcass there, so I hauled it back by towing it behind my kayak. The Inupiat are allowed to kill polar bears, but according to our laws, the carcass must be registered with the Fish and Wildlife Service. And we are not allowed to waste a kill. Anyway, Theo heard about it and wanted to have a look first. It was only when he made his exam that we found out she had cubs somewhere."

Lukie sighed. "We never hunt mother bears. We want to keep the bear population high."

"Could you show us where it happened on a map?" Ben asked, smiling. "You should put a flag or something there to mark your brave encounter."

Lukie smiled. "Follow me," he said. He led them to one of the maps they had seen outside the entrance to the center. "This is our most recent map of the local ice cover," he said. He lifted his finger and pointed at a spot on the map. "And I was here."

To Ben and Zoe's surprise, Lukie did not point to anywhere on land. Instead his finger went straight to the north side of a large island of ice, separated from Fairwood by a wide channel of water.

"I was here on this floe," Lukie said, tapping the map. "That spur that sticks out to the north. I always find a good supply of codfish there."

"But that's just floating ice," Ben said, surprised. "I thought bears built birthing dens on the mainland. What was she doing out there?"

"A few bears make their dens in the snow banks on the ice floes," said Lukie.

The saleswoman waved at him from the door. "Lukie!" she called. "There's a delivery of guidebooks. I need your help carrying them!"

Lukie gave them a grin and left to help. Ben peered closely at the map, memorizing the coordinates of the area. He entered them into his BUG. "This will make the search much easier," he said.

Zoe's shoulders slumped. "It will be difficult to reach that ice floe," she said. "The Arctic Ocean is in the way."

Zoe and Ben gazed out over the bleak stretch of icy water. "This mission's going to be much more dangerous than we thought," Ben said.

CHAPTER 5

TROUBLED WATERS

Zoe and Ben had their hoods up and goggles on against the cold as they paddled their kayaks across the gray, choppy water. They were heading for the ice floe off the shore. "This is such a cool way to travel!" Zoe said.

Ben glanced down at the frigid water beneath him. "Yeah, it's cool, all right," he said. "*Too* cool. It won't be much fun if we fall in the water."

As soon as they told Erika that they
needed to get to the floe, she had rented
two kayaks from the visitor center. Erika
gave the owner a cover story — they'd be
away exploring the area for a few days.
Once they left Fairwood, their "mother"
headed up the coast where the oil drilling
was taking place.

Meanwhile, Zoe and Ben were headed for the ice floe.

Zoe skillfully steered a path through the floating obstacles. "These kayaks would be really fast if there wasn't so much ice in the water," she said "Good thing we practiced canoeing in our WILD training."

In some places, the ice was in flat pieces that looked like shattered mirrors. In other places, the ice formed natural ice sculptures that towered above Zoe and Ben, glinting in the afternoon sunlight.

Ben slipped his BUG out of his pocket. "Good thing Uncle Stephen gave us these special thin gloves," he said. "We'd never hit the right buttons if our fingers were covered with wool." He brought up the satellite map. "We're heading in the right direction. About another twenty minutes of kayaking and we'll reach the southern tip of the ice floe. Then we have a trek across it."

"A trek?" Zoe repeated. "More like a race! I can't wait to try out my RAT."

"There's a problem up ahead," Ben said suddenly.

Ben pointed at his BUG. "The satellite picture shows we'll be passing through a thick fog," he said. "It'll be hard to see — and much colder."

Soon they saw a bank of white dense vapor swirling on the surface of the sea in front of them. There didn't seem to be any way around it. "Luckily we have our BUGs to guide us," Zoe said. "Otherwise, we'd end up going around in circles."

They paddled into the thick fog. It was impossible to see much farther than the end of the kayak. "Stay close," Ben said.

They made their way through the thick, freezing air. The paddling kept them warm, but they could feel droplets of ice clinging to their hoods and masks. The only noise was the splash of their oars and the clunking sound of ice blocks clashing together.

Zoe was paddling as close to Ben as she could to keep him in sight. "I'll be relieved when we reach the floe," she said.

Ben nodded. "Me too," he said. "This is kind of creepy."

Something dark loomed ahead in the fog. The children slowed their kayaks. "What's that?" Zoe whispered. "It looks like a row of gray people wearing hoods . . . and they're crouched down. I don't like it."

Now they could hear sounds, as if someone was tapping on wood. Zoe back-paddled as fast as she could.

"It can't be humans," Ben said, trying to sound brave. He tapped a key on his BUG to identify the sound. When the result flashed up on the screen, he burst out laughing. "Don't worry," he said to his sister. "It's just a pod of walruses on the ice floe."

The fog cleared a little. In the small shaft of sunlight that glowed upon the ice floe, Ben and Zoe could see the walruses lying on the edge of the ice. Their pinkish-gray bodies were covered in short hair, and their snouts bristled with stiff whiskers. Each one had a pair of gleaming tusks that pointed downward.

With an embarrassed grin on her face, Zoe paddled her kayak back to Ben. "Well, they looked pretty scary back there," she said.

"Honestly, they still look kind of scary," Ben said, chuckling. "I know they don't usually attack humans, but those tusks look mighty sharp."

"You're probably right," Zoe said. "We should go around them and land on the other side."

One of the walruses was watching them carefully with its beady eyes. It turned its head to follow their movements, its snout raised into the air, whiskers twitching. Suddenly it gave a harsh, bellowing cry. The other animals joined it, and they all began to shuffle toward the sea.

"They've caught our scent," said Ben, plunging his paddle into the water. "We should have used the scent dispersers on our BUGs, but it's too late now. Get away as fast as you can. Walruses always jump into the water when they're frightened."

Just as he spoke, the walruses plunged into the icy ocean with tremendous speed. Waves of water surged against the kayaks. Ben and Zoe rowed as fast as they could back into the fog, but more animals were diving into the sea.

Shiny walrus heads were popping up all over the place. They let out terrified cries as they swam away.

Zoe let out a yelp as a wave of water tipped her sideways. Ben twisted in his seat to try to grab his sister through the wall of fog, but she was just out of reach. Zoe drifted to the side, holding out her hand. In a moment, she was nowhere to be seen.

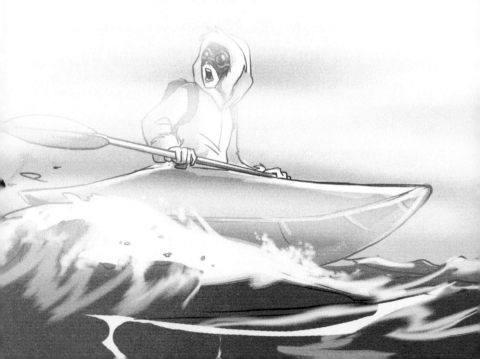

CHAPTER 6

WHITEOUT

"Zoe!" Ben called out. His voice sounded muffled in the fog. "Zoe, where are you?!"

Ben listened. All he heard was the crunch and grind of floating ice as it bumped into the kayak. His heart was racing. He knew that if Zoe had tipped over, she wouldn't survive long in the freezing Arctic water.

Ben began to paddle around, scanning the choppy waves. Nothing. Hands shaking with fear, he steered the kayak through the ice, looking right and left.

"Zoe!" Ben called out again. This time, he heard the rising panic in his own voice. "Where are you?!"

Then at last he heard a call — so faint that he thought he was imagining it. Then he heard it again. Ben quickly propelled the kayak through the swirling fog toward the sound.

As Ben passed through the fog, he saw the outline of a figure on the edge of the ice floe. It was waving frantically. "Ben!" Zoe called.

Ben breathed a sigh of relief. He swiftly brought his kayak up to the bank of ice. Zoe was kneeling, her hand stretched toward him to help him climb out.

Ben pulled his lightweight craft out of the water and put it next to his sister's. "I thought you capsized!" cried Ben.

"I almost did!" Zoe said. "Remember that capsize training session we did with canoes?"

Ben nodded. "You were really good at it," he admitted.

"Lucky for me," said Zoe. "Every time I felt myself tipping over, I slapped the water with the paddle and twisted upward. As soon as the all the walruses left, I climbed onto the ice. It was scary, Ben."

Ben hugged his sister. "Well, we're both okay now," he said, smiling at her. "But we have to be more careful."

"Agreed," said Zoe, her voice still tense. "Let's get away from the water."

"First we have to fit our trackers to the kayaks," Ben said. "Then we'll be able to locate them wherever we end up."

BUG SAT MAP

KEY
////// = SNOW RIDGES

N

ARCTIC OCEAN

FAIRWOOD

MAIN STREET

INUP
HERIT
CENTE

Zoe detached a small gadget from her BUG and clipped it to the kayak. Ben did the same with his. Then they turned the kayaks over and covered them with snow.

Ben checked the screen of his BUG. An orange light pulsed. "The tracker's working," he said. He tapped some more keys to bring up a local map of the area.

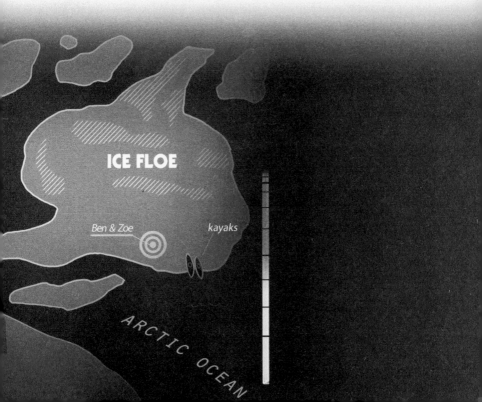

ICE FLOE

Ben & Zoe

kayaks

ARCTIC OCEAN

"I'm checking the coordinates from the map Lukie showed us," he told Zoe. Ben studied the map on his screen, then pointed. "It's that way."

"Northward!" Zoe said, smiling.

"Time for the RATs," Ben said excitedly. They both pulled their slim snowboards out of the side pockets of their backpacks and dropped them onto the snow.

Ben and Zoe pressed their heels onto the starting buttons and the RAT motors whirred to life. Off they went, weaving two parallel tracks in the untouched snow.

They looked toward their destination. At their feet, the ice floe was covered in a smooth layer of snow.

Farther down, the ice had been sculpted into strange shapes by the wind. Some formations made gentle mounds. Others looked like jagged ledges that were covered with overhanging snow.

Ben surged ahead. "Watch this!" he yelled back to his sister. He steered the RAT toward a hump in the ground and jumped off it, balancing expertly in the air with outstretched arms. "Olympic jump!" he boasted. He landed several feet away.

With a look of determination on her face, Zoe copied him. She glanced back at the two landing marks in the snow and grinned. She had jumped farther. "You only get the silver medal," she said. "Because I won the gold!"

Zoe zoomed after her brother. Ben slowed a little, then checked to see if Zoe was close behind.

Then Ben stamped down with his heel on the back of his RAT. The end dug into the snow, sending a powdery white spray flying up behind him — and all over Zoe.

Ben burst out laughing as he zoomed away, with Zoe on his tail. But suddenly Ben brought his RAT to a halt. Zoe just managed to avoid colliding with him. "A joke's a joke," she said crossly, "but I almost ran into you just now."

"Sorry," said Ben. "But check out the sky up ahead."

Zoe stared up at the horizon. Gray clouds were swirling around in the distance. The clouds were getting closer and the wind was whipping the snow around their feet.

"That's bad," Zoe said. "It looks like the snowstorm we heard about. That's definitely going to make it harder to find the cubs."

The low sun was now completely blotted out by the dark clouds. Flakes of snow were falling fast and being driven straight into their faces by the wind. Ben and Zoe wouldn't be able to keep their balance on the RATs. "We'll have to walk the rest of the way," said Ben.

"I can't see a thing," Zoe yelled as they trudged along. "And it's getting colder. I'm not sure how much farther I can go."

"This is hopeless," said Ben. "Let's get the tent up. We'll have to sit out the storm or we'll just get lost."

Ben reached into his backpack and pulled out the folded tent. Together they tried to open it, but the blustering wind kept pulling it from their grasp. The thin material was slipping through their gloved hands like a wet fish.

"Don't let go!" Ben yelled to Zoe.

But it was too late. A vicious blast of wind tore the tent out of their hands. It whipped and twisted across the tundra until it was a tiny dot on the horizon.

CHAPTER 7

SHELTER

"Now what are we going to do?" Ben asked desperately. "We'll never survive out here in a snowstorm without shelter."

Zoe realized something. "Remember what Amaguq said about snow holes?" she asked. "We need to make one — now!"

Ben pointed into the distance. "The ground looks raised over there," he said. "There might be enough snow to dig into."

"It's hard to see anything!" shouted Zoe.

Zoe was struggling to walk against the rising strength of the wind as it howled around them and tugged at their clothes.

At last they reached the bank of snow. They dropped to their knees, the wind blasting into their faces.

"Perfect!" yelled Ben. "It's facing away from the wind!"

"I wish we were!" Zoe yelled back.

They clawed blindly at the snow. "It's falling too fast to clear!" Ben said.

"Use your RAT as a shovel!" Zoe suggested. Together, they scooped up big shovelfuls of snow with the boards.

A few minutes later, they had scooped out a space just big enough to crawl into. They lay huddled together in their sleeping bags, listening to the wind roaring outside.

Zoe pulled a flashlight out of her backpack. She shined its beam at the entrance to their shelter. It lit the snowflakes that were driving past the entrance. The storm was raging.

"It's unbelievable," said Ben. "We've seen snowstorms like this on TV, but I never realized how bad it would be to get caught in the middle of one."

"It's going to delay our search," said Zoe. "Those poor cubs."

Ben sighed. "It could go on for hours," he said. "We'll have to make the best of it. How about some food? I'm hungry."

Zoe laughed. "You're always hungry," she said. Wriggling around, she slipped her hand into her brother's backpack. "If you get your elbow out of my stomach, I might be able to reach the food."

"Fine," Ben said. He shifted his body and then yelped. "Great, now I'm sitting on the RAT's motor." Zoe chuckled.

Soon, they both had their high-energy fruit bars unwrapped. They sat and munched in silence. Outside, it was as dark as night, and the snow was piling up over the hole's entrance.

Strange noises rose up above the whine of the wind. "That's the ice floe creaking," said Zoe. "It moves all the time, but this storm is making it worse." She scooped some snow into her glove and sucked at it. "At least we have plenty of water."

Ben yawned and rubbed his eyes. "I'm going to get some sleep," he told Zoe. "Wake me up when the storm's over."

Zoe nodded. She knew she wouldn't be able to sleep anyway. Her mind was too busy picturing the shivering bear cubs alone in their den. She wondered how she and Ben would ever get to them in time. Any tracks the mother polar bear or fisherman had left would be covered in fresh snow. And so would the den.

Zoe's breathing quickened and her thoughts grew rushed. She started to feel really confused.

Zoe turned to Ben. She was horrified to see that his lips were blue, but when she touched his skin, it felt warm. What was happening?

She shook her brother hard. She was relieved to see he was breathing, but he wouldn't wake up. She tried to concentrate, but she felt so light-headed! She took a handful of snow and rubbed it in her face to wake herself up.

Zoe swung the flashlight around. *Where's the entrance to the shelter?* she thought. It had vanished. *Am I having a nightmare?* She shook her head. *No, that's silly, I'm obviously awake.*

Then Zoe realized what was happening. The storm had sealed them in. They were trapped in a tomb of snow. If the hole was gone, then no air was getting inside. They were slowly suffocating!

Zoe knew she had to do something right away. Soon, she would pass out from the lack of oxygen. All she wanted to do was close her eyes and fall sleep. "Stay awake!" she muttered to herself. She pinched her cheeks hard, hoping the pain would keep her alert.

Zoe started to scrape at the covered entrance, but the snow was thick and her strength had already drained away. She gasped from the lack of air as she clawed desperately against the walls.

Just when Zoe thought she couldn't dig anymore, the snow fell away and her gloved hand broke through the wall. With the last of her strength, Zoe heaved herself up to the small gap and took great gulps of freezing air. She felt her brain slowly grow clearer. She twisted around to Ben.

He was pale and still. Zoe's heart almost stopped. "Wake up, Ben!" Zoe cried. She tugged at her brother's jacket and managed to drag him toward the small hole. His head fell forward. He wasn't moving.

CHAPTER 8

STRANGE LIGHTS

"Ben, wake up!" Zoe cried. She rubbed hard on his back. Then she shook him. But nothing was working. Desperately, she took a handful of snow and shoved it into his face.

Ben gave a faint groan and his eyelids fluttered. "What's your problem!" he mumbled.

Zoe didn't hesitate. She got another handful of snow and rubbed it over his face.

"Stop it!" Ben said. He was trying to turn his head away, but he was still dazed and confused from the lack of oxygen.

"Breathe deeply," Zoe insisted, slapping his cheeks. "You lost consciousness for a while."

Gradually, Ben came around. To Zoe's relief, his skin began to grow more pink, although his eyes were still heavy and he slumped back against the wall of the snow hole. She put an energy bar into his hand and watched him slowly chew it.

"What happened?" Ben asked groggily.

"Our entrance got covered with snow and we didn't make an air hole," Zoe explained. "We were slowly suffocating."

"I bet polar bears remember to leave an air hole when they build a den," Ben said.

"We have to start searching for the cubs' den as soon as you feel better," said Zoe. "I can't hear the wind anymore."

Ben dug at the entrance until it was wide enough for him to see through. "It's dark out there!" he said. "We must have been in here for hours."

Zoe checked outside. "It stopped snowing," she said. "Let's go."

They pulled their goggles back on, busted out of their shelter, and took in the dark landscape. The snow clouds had gone as quickly as they'd come. A pale moon was high in the sky, turning the sky an inky blue. The children switched on small flashlights that were stitched into the front of their masks.

"Visibility is okay," Zoe said. A light flashed on her BUG screen.

"We're close to where the attack happened," Ben said. "The den shouldn't be too far away." He pressed a key on his BUG and an arrow flashed on the screen. "Follow me."

They both jumped onto their RATs and sped across the new, powdery snow, stopping every now and then to check the direction. Zoe slowed down her RAT. "It looks like the ground is moving just ahead," she said.

Ben looked up ahead. "That's the ocean," he said. "It's the floating ice that you can see moving. Handy little BUG, it hasn't let us down yet."

Zoe looked around. "It's a lot wider than I expected," she said.

They jumped off their boards, folded them, and stuck them back in their backpacks.

Ben tapped some keys. "I've set it to look for the thickest snow banks," he said. "That has to be where the den is."

"Time for thermal imaging," Zoe said. She pressed the logo on the side of her snow goggles. At once, the bottom half of the lenses became cloudy. As she looked at Ben, she could see his face clearly. However, his legs showed up as a purple, yellow, and orange glow. "With some luck, we'll pick up the cubs' body heat."

If they're still alive, Zoe thought.

Ben clicked his goggles, turning on thermal mode. "There's a long ridge of snow forty feet from here," he said. "Let's start our search there."

Reaching the ridge, they moved along slowly, staring intently through their goggles.

There was no sign of the glowing shape of a warm, living body anywhere. "They're not here," Ben said. He tapped at one key and then another on his BUG. "That's strange. I can't seem to update this map. The screen seems to be frozen."

"Mine's stuck, too," Zoe said, surprised. "Do you think it's too cold for them?" She pressed the hot key that contacted WILD Headquarters. "I'll ask Uncle Stephen." She gave the BUG a shake. "Great, that's not working either. This is scary, Ben. How will we be able to find our kayaks again, or contact HQ?"

"This is really strange," said Ben. "I'm sure Uncle Stephen said he adapted our BUGs for cold conditions. We'll just have to keep searching and worry about the rest later."

Ben scanned the snowy ground, looking for possible den sites. "The blizzard hasn't made our job any easier," said Zoe. "The snow will have covered any tracks."

"Let's look for another ridge," suggested Ben. "The den has to be somewhere near here."

They trudged across the snow until a high bank came into view. "Look!" Zoe said, pointing at a small hole. "My goggles picked up something living inside there."

"It's about the right size for a cub," Ben said excitedly.

"Wait," Zoe warned him. "That's not a very big entrance. I don't think a mother polar bear would fit."

Ben had already stuck his hand inside.

He turned to look at Zoe just as a snarl rang out from inside the hole. An angry animal darted past him and disappeared into the darkness.

"Yikes!" Ben said, gasping. "What was that?"

"It was an Arctic fox," Zoe said. Ben let out a sigh of relief.

"This is hopeless," Zoe said. "How are we going to find the den without our BUGs?"

"I have an idea," said Ben. "We can see where we've been from our footprints, right?" Zoe nodded. "Well, let's keep the moon behind us and move up the floe. It'll be slow going, but it should work."

Zoe nodded. They set off walking toward the direction of the moon. They seemed to trudge on for hours, getting colder by the minute. Suddenly, Zoe looked up with a puzzled look on her face. Ben followed her gaze — and saw something beautiful up in the sky.

Before their astonished eyes, the glow grew into an arc of vivid green light that streaked across the sky. Ben and Zoe watched in silence, mesmerized by the long shimmering curtains of light weaving their way through the dark sky. The colors swirled and flashed above their heads.

Zoe couldn't look away. "Why is there a purple glow ahead on the horizon?" she asked, still staring skyward.

To Zoe's surprise, Ben was grinning from ear to ear. "Don't be scared," he explained. "It's the aurora borealis."

"The northern lights!" cried Zoe. "Of course! That's awesome! I've seen pictures of it, but I never thought it'd be this beautiful."

They gazed upward as yellow ribbons of light danced across the sky.

Waving beams of red and green flashed across the horizon. At times, it seemed to Zoe and Ben that giant faces and shapes appeared in the billowing colors.

"Now I can see why there are stories about gods being seen in the sky," Zoe said.

Ben grinned. "Actually, the lights are caused by particles from the sun colliding with the oxygen and nitrogen atoms in the atmosphere," he explained.

"Thanks, Mr. Walking Encyclopedia," Zoe said, rolling her eyes at Ben. "Don't you have any imagination?"

Then Zoe gasped. "I think I know why our BUGs stopped working!" she said. "It must be all this electrical activity." She scanned the area. "And look how well it's lighting up the ground."

"You're right," Ben said, pointing eagerly. "I can see a tall bank of snow ahead."

Zoe nodded and smiled hopefully. "That would be the perfect place for a polar bear den," she said.

They jumped on to their RATs and zipped toward the snowbank. The shiny surface shimmered with the reflected glow from above. "Thank you, northern lights," Zoe yelled up at the sky. "We can see really well now. Sorry we can't stay to watch the whole show."

They skidded to a stop where the bank began, sending up a shower of snow in their wakes. "It's much bigger than I thought," said Ben. He looked up and down the long ridge through his thermogoggles.

"It'll take hours to search all of these ridges," Ben said.

"I have an idea," said Zoe. "If it's the weird electricity of the aurora borealis that's interfering with the BUGs, then it might only be their satellite function that's affected." She clicked a few buttons on her BUG, then let out a cheer in triumph. "I was right!" she said. "Look, the scent disperser still works and the animal cry analysis is functioning."

"Great," Ben said. "We can set that to pick up the cubs' call. It has a much wider range than the thermogoggles."

Zoe looked up to see a fading red glow in the distance. "The lights are getting fainter," she said. "It'll be dark again soon. We have to search quickly while there's still some light."

They moved along the bank, scanning every inch of snow with the goggles and checking their BUGs for any indication of cubs. The glow in the sky was disappearing fast. Soon they were relying on their headlamps and the pale moonlight to find their way.

Zoe stopped and held up her BUG. It was flashing. "It detected a polar bear cub cry," she said excitedly.

"Where's it coming from?" said Ben.

"That's strange," said Zoe, frowning. "It can't be coming from a den. The cry's far away from the bank." She spun around and pointed at a jagged point of ice that rose up from the snow. "Behind there, I think."

Ben set off quickly, his boots sending up sprays of snow as he ran.

"Slow down," warned Zoe. "You don't want to scare it."

As they rounded the point of ice, Zoe saw something in the beam from her headlamp. "It's a tiny bear cub!" Zoe cried.

CHAPTER 9

SLURPY AND POKEY

The little white bundle of fur was curled up in the snow. "The poor little thing," said Zoe. "It must be one of the orphans. It left the den looking for its mom."

"Is it still alive?" Ben asked anxiously.

"I can see its chest moving," Zoe said. She quickly pulled the fleece sling out of her backpack. "Help me slip the bear into the sling." Zoe bent over the cub. "We've got to warm you up!"

"You'd be better off growling at it," Ben said, unfolding the sling. "We've got to act like its mom, remember?"

Zoe lifted the little cub up. Just like Uncle Stephen said, it was about the size of a large cat. Its dark eyes blinked at Zoe. "It's a girl," she said. She laid the cub onto the fleece and gently wrapped it around her. The cub let out a mewing sound as it nuzzled into the fur.

Ben helped Zoe gently put the sling on so that the bear was secure against her chest. All of a sudden, Zoe felt something tug at her glove. The little cub was sucking noisily at the end of one of her fingers.

"We'll get you some food as soon as we can," Zoe said. "But first we're going to check your den to see if you've got any brothers or sisters."

"Pass me your BUG," Ben said. "I'll set it to emit a female polar bear scent so that Junior here thinks you're her mom."

Zoe handed it over. As she did, she caught sight of tiny footprints in the snow.

The little prints had five claws and led across the snow toward the far end of the bank. "Look, here are her tracks," Zoe said. "The long ones are the front paws. Five pads and claws on each print. She must have come out after the storm."

They started to follow the trail. The prints led them to the ridge in a wobbly line. The little cub began to wriggle and grunt.

"I think she's warming up," said Zoe, "and getting hungry. We'll have to feed her soon."

After a few minutes they came to a dip in the bank. Looking through the thermal part of their goggles, Ben and Zoe could see a faint orange and purple glow from deep inside the snow.

"I think we found another polar bear cub!" Zoe said.

"There's a tunnel here," Ben said, brushing away the snow. "I'm going to explore."

"Don't get stuck," said Zoe.

"No chance," said Ben, grinning. "It has to be wide enough for an adult polar bear, remember? They're a lot fatter than I am."

He got down on his belly and shuffled into the hole until Zoe could only see the soles of his boots. Then his feet disappeared inside. Zoe watched anxiously at the entrance. Eventually, Ben's smiling face reappeared.

"Got it!" Ben cried. "It's very weak, but it still tried to bite me just like the fox." He examined his glove and grinned. "Good old Uncle Stephen. Not only are these gloves ultra-thin, they're nibble-proof, as well."

Ben began to go back down the tunnel, feet first. He gestured for Zoe to join him. "It's warmer in here than out there," he called. "Just the place for feeding time."

Zoe crawled in quickly. There was room for her to crawl on her hands and knees so she didn't have to undo the sling. The tunnel gave way to a small chamber. Ben was putting the new cub into its fleece.

"It's another girl," he told Zoe. "She's smaller than her sister and not as strong."

"But we've got them!" Zoe squealed with delight. "I was beginning to think this was one WILD mission that was going to end in tragedy."

"It's not over until we bring them back," Ben said.

"And they'll need food before we head out," said Zoe.

Zoe unpacked the bottles and dried milk. After stuffing snow into a bottle, she melted it with a small battery-operated heater. When it was warm, she added a packet of dried milk. The cubs caught the scent and began to squeal and wriggle. Zoe quickly attached nipples to the bottles and handed one of them to Ben.

"Better give it to them slowly," Zoe warned as her cub drank quickly. "It will be a shock to their empty tummies."

Ben tried to release the bottle from his cub's mouth. "I'm going to call this one Slurpy," he said. "She slurps every time she drinks. She may be small and weak, but she's determined to survive."

"My cub won't stop poking its nose into everything I do," said Zoe, scratching her furry head. "Pokey is the name for you."

She looked around the den. The walls were smooth, with a claw mark here and there where the mother had dug. "It's warm in here," said Zoe.

Ben grinned. "Yep, this is pretty luxurious," he said. "Compared to our little snow hole, anyway."

As soon as the cubs had finished drinking, Zoe crawled out of the tunnel. She shivered as the freezing outside air hit her in the face. "Time for the homeward journey," she said.

Zoe checked the satellite function on her BUG. "Hey!" she called to Ben as he emerged. "It's working again. We'll be able to find our way back to the kayaks using the trackers."

"I think your theory about the interference was right," said Ben, fiddling with his BUG. "Now that the northern lights have stopped, everything's fine."

Zoe stepped onto her RAT. "It's almost too bad," she said with a sigh. "The lights were such a fantastic show."

They checked to make sure that their cubs were comfortable.

Then Ben and Zoe set off on their RATs along the ice toward the main floe.

Zoe sped along in front of Ben. "It's a lot harder to balance with a polar bear cub around your shoulders!" she shouted to her brother.

Ben didn't reply. Zoe turned. Ben had stopped a way back and was looking around. "I can hear a boat," he called to Zoe.

Zoe could hear it too. It sounded like the deep, throbbing hum of an engine. Then she saw it in the distance. It was a cruise ship, emitting a glow of golden light from every window. It seemed to be heading very close to the floe. Behind thick glass windows, they could see people dancing at a late night party.

Zoe ducked down behind the ridge. She quickly turned off her headlamp. "Hide!" she yelled. "We can't be seen." Ben found a jagged ice formation and squatted in its shadow.

The throbbing noise grew louder. The ice beneath them began to shake. *Just how close is this ship going to come?* thought Ben. *If it plows through the ice, we'll be doomed.*

The ship towered above them as it glided slowly past the ice floe. The rumbling of its engines was deafening. The reverberations shook their bodies, making the cubs whimper in fear.

Suddenly, there was a terrible crash. A fierce crack ran along the ice. A dark, jagged line zigzagged over the snow in front of Ben. The spur of ice was breaking away from the main floe, leaving Zoe on one side and him on the other.

Ben was stranded.

CHAPTER 10

WILD RIDE

Ben and Zoe stared in horror at the widening channel of freezing Arctic water between them.

"Stay there!" shouted Zoe. "I'll go and get a kayak."

"No," Ben shouted back. "By the time you return, I could have already drifted miles away from here. Don't worry, I've got a plan."

"You're not going to do anything stupid, right?" called Zoe.

Ben didn't reply. Instead, he turned his RAT and steered away from the broken edge of the spur.

"Where are you going?" Zoe cried out in alarm.

"Stand back," Ben shouted. He brought the RAT to a halt and swung it 180 degrees in the snow so that he was facing Zoe once again. With a look of grim determination on his face, he revved up the motor. Then he took off, accelerating until he was racing at top speed toward the water.

Zoe suddenly realized what her daredevil brother was about to do. He was going to jump the gap! "No!" she shrieked. "You'll never make it!"

But it was too late. Ben was already crouching on his board, both arms stretched out for balance.

Zoe could hardly watch as he sprang up into the air toward her, the whirring RAT beneath his feet. It was a huge jump, and was made even more difficult by the weight of the cub in Ben's sling.

For a moment, it looked as if Ben was
going to plunge straight into the freezing
depths. Desperately, Ben waved his arms
to get his balance, then lurched forward.
Zoe let out a scream as her brother flew
through the air.

Ben landed hard on the edge of the ice. A loud cracking noise ripped through the air as the ice began to fall away into the water. Ben, the cub, and his RAT tumbled onto the ice. But they were safe.

Zoe darted over to him. Ben got to his knees, made sure he hadn't squashed Slurpy, and raised his hand for a high-five.

"You're insane!" cried his sister. She helped pull Ben to his feet. Zoe took a deep breath. "But I guess you get the Olympic gold this time."

"It was nothing," Ben said, grinning. "But you can have my autograph later."

Ben wasn't going to admit that he'd felt as scared as Zoe had looked. He didn't like to think of what would have happened to him — and the cub — if he hadn't made it.

Ben stroked Slurpy, and the little cub popped her head up. She began to wriggle around, trying to get out of the sling. "I don't blame you, Slurpy!" said Ben. "That was a wild ride."

The children checked the kayak tracker, then raced off across the ice floe. Their headlamps lit the way as they traveled.

The storm had blown the snow into frozen ripples. There were a few animal tracks trailing across it.

Zoe cut a sharp turn and came up alongside Ben, spraying him with an arc of powdery snow. "Couldn't resist," Zoe said. "If we got snow like this at home, we'd be out all day making snowmen and having snowball fights and sledding." She trailed off when she noticed that Ben was frowning. "What's the matter?" Zoe asked.

"I'm worried about Slurpy," Ben said.

"Does she seem sick?" asked Zoe.

"No," Ben said. "She wants to get out. Her squirming is messing with my balance!"

Zoe laughed. "It's not much farther," she said. In the moonlight, the kayaks' snowy outlines were just visible in the distance. "Look, there are our kayaks. Soon, we'll get Slurpy and Pokey to someone who can take care of them."

"Top speed!" yelled Ben, smiling again.

But Zoe had come to a stop. "There's something else near the edge of the floe," she said, pointing at a large, dark shape in the snow.

"Nothing to worry about," Ben said. "It's just a lump of ice . . . isn't it?"

Zoe gulped. "Lumps of ice can't walk," she said slowly. "It's coming toward us, Ben. It's a polar bear."

Ben's eyes went wide. "You're right," he said. He brought his RAT to a halt. "Wave your arms and make yourself as tall as possible. Try not to seem scared."

Zoe did as Ben said, although she could feel her heart thumping in fear. The huge polar bear raised its head to the sky and gave a ferocious growl. "I hope it's not hungry," she whispered.

"We have to show it we're human — and dominant," Ben told her quickly. "Go away!" he yelled in his deepest voice. Zoe joined in. But the bear began to pad toward them.

"It's not working," Zoe said, trying to keep the fear out of her voice.

The bear galloped toward them. Its strong legs pounded away at the snow and its sharp teeth gleamed in the moonlight. It was covering the gap between them quickly — too quickly. Now, it wasn't only the cubs that needed to be saved.

CHAPTER 11

RAT RACE

Then, Zoe thought of something. It was crazy, but it just might work. "Go!" she yelled to Ben. "Use your RAT and escape!" She turned so that her board was facing away from their advancing attacker.

"Even on these we can't move faster than a bear!" Ben said.

"Just trust me!" Zoe screamed. "I'll be right behind you, I promise."

Ben knew better than to argue. "You'd better be," he said.

Ben jumped on his RAT, clutched Slurpy tight to his chest, and darted away at full speed.

Trying to keep calm, Zoe kicked her RAT into action. The bear was almost to her. It reared up, massive front paws raised, ready to crush her. Zoe tipped the back of the RAT into the snow and revved hard, just like Ben had done earlier. At once, the motor caught on the soft snow and sent up a thick spray straight into the face of the bear. It recoiled with a frightened growl.

Zoe didn't waste a second. She moved her weight forward and chased after her brother. Every now and then, she shifted her back foot to kick up a thick mist of snow behind her.

When Zoe peeked over her shoulder, she couldn't see the bear. She caught up with Ben. "I think it gave up the chase," Zoe said.

Ben nodded. He stopped and scanned behind them for animal noises. The BUG detected no polar bears — except for Slurpy and Pokey, of course. "Nice work, Zoe," he said. "I thought we were going to be that bear's breakfast! But let's get out of here quickly in case it decides to come back."

They dug their kayaks out of the snow and climbed into them right on the edge of the ice. Then they launched themselves with a splash into the icy water.

When they had paddled away from the ice, Ben brought up the satellite map.

"I don't need that map to tell me which way to go," said Zoe.

She pointed over to where the sky was illuminated with the pink glow of dawn. "That's the east and we want to head south," she said.

"You're such an expert guide," Ben said, grinning. "The Inupiat people will be begging you to stay."

Zoe stuck out her tongue at him. Then she checked her little cub and laughed. "Pokey has no idea what we've been through for her," she said. "She's fast asleep."

"So is Slurpy," Ben said. He sighed. "At last."

"Let's find out where to take them," Zoe said, hitting the key on her BUG that called WILD HQ.

"Hello there!" Uncle Stephen's voice boomed out. "What do you have to report?"

"We found two cubs," Zoe said.

"Good work!" their uncle cried out. "There's a polar bear rehabilitation center a few miles down the coast from Fairwood."

Zoe's BUG showed a new set of coordinates. "That's its location," said Uncle Stephen. "It's called the Puyuk Shelter. You can take your little cubs there."

"What's our cover story?" asked Zoe. "We can't tell them the truth."

"Hmmm," Uncle Stephen said. Zoe could picture her uncle rubbing his chin as he thought. "I believe a 'leaving it on the doorstep' scenario would be best. Just place the cubs by the entrance, ring the bell, and run like mad!"

SAFE AND SOUND

The bright morning sun was shining down on the Arctic ocean as Ben and Zoe walked along the beach back to Fairwood. As soon as they'd made sure that the cubs were safely in the Puyuk shelter, they snuck back to their kayaks and paddled away. Erika was on her way to meet them in the village.

"Hi there, kids!" came a familiar voice. "You're awake early!" It was Lukie, dragging his kayak down the beach to the water.

Zoe and Ben ran over to him. "I see you've got your backpacks," said Lukie eagerly. "Going off on an adventure?"

"Just being here is an adventure!" Ben said, keeping up their cover. "It's a fantastic place. I wish we were staying longer, but our mother will be whisking us away any minute now."

"Where are you going next?" asked the fisherman.

Ben looked blank, so Zoe jumped in. "Mom likes to surprise us," she said with a smile. "It's a sort of mystery tour." She glanced at the gear in his boat. "Are you going fishing?"

"I am," said Lukie. "I'm really glad I didn't risk it yesterday. That was one terrible storm that came through. Did you hear it?"

"We certainly did!" Ben said, a wide grin on his face.

"You wouldn't have wanted to be out in it, I can tell you!" Lukie said. "But today is perfect for fishing." He jerked a thumb toward the road that led down to the water. "I think your taxi arrived."

Ben and Zoe looked behind them. A dog sled, driven by Charlie, was gliding along the road. Erika was in the back of the sled, waving at them.

"Have a great trip!" Lukie said.

"You too," replied Zoe. "Hope you don't meet any more bears!"

Lukie laughed. "So do I!" he said, waving at Ben and Zoe as they ran away toward their taxi.

* * *

Later that day, back at WILD HQ, Ben and Zoe watched anxiously as Uncle Stephen brought up the Puyuk Shelter website on his computer. They were wasting no time in checking on the cubs' progress.

"I won't ever forget that moment," Zoe said as the site was loading. "When we put the cubs down on the front step and rang the bell . . ."

". . . we realized they were still inside our fleece slings!" Ben said, continuing his sister's sentence. "We knew we couldn't leave any clues about WILD behind, so we sprinted back to them and took them out."

"And then Pokey started to wander away!" Zoe said, laughing. "I had to chase her down and put her back on the doorstep."

The website finished loading. Their godfather clicked on the "news" tab. "'Amazing find,'" he read aloud, winking at Ben and Zoe. "'Two cubs turned up on our doorstep yesterday morning. It's a miracle they were found alive.'"

"Scroll down, Uncle Stephen," Ben urged. "I want to find out how Slurpy is."

"The cubs were given the names Slurpy and Pokey in a note left behind by their anonymous saviors," Uncle Stephen read aloud. "The cubs were missing their mom, but with a bit of tender loving care, they are now eating well and these two little cubs will soon have a new foster mother bear."

"Awesome!" said Ben. He looked at Zoe. "And I admit, Slurpy was pretty cute."

Zoe playfully punched Ben in the shoulder. "And you say I'm the one who's always geeking out over cute animals!" she said.

"You are," said Ben. He chuckled. "You get the gold medal in cuteness overload every time. I'm just happy they found another mother for the cubs."

"That's what we're here for," Uncle Stephen said with a smile. He continued to read the article. "'We have no idea who the cubs' human rescuers were,'" he read aloud. "'We only saw your boot tracks and the note you left behind with the cubs' names — but thank you, whoever you might be!'"

"And thank you from us, too," said Erika, giving the children a hug. "I'm very proud to have been your mother for a few days."

Zoe laughed. "Don't get all mushy on us, Mom," she joked.

"Hey, Zoe," Ben said, turning back to the screen. "Here's an idea for a summer vacation trip. They do tourist visits at the center. We can go and see Pokey and Slurpy!"

"Great idea!" cried Zoe. "I'd love to see them again."

"Even better," Ben said, pointing at the screen. He grinned mischievously. "It says here we can even swim with the bears, separated only by a thin sheet of glass."

Zoe laughed nervously. "No, thanks," she said. "I'll stick with the cute, harmless little cubs."

Ben chuckled, then nodded. "You're right," he said. "I never want to come that close to an adult polar bear again!"

THE AUTHORS

Jan Burchett and **Sara Vogler** were already friends when they discovered they both wanted to write children's books, and that it was much more fun to do it together. They have since written over a hundred and thirty stories ranging from educational books and stories for younger readers to young adult fiction. They have written for series such as Dinosaur Cove and Beast Quest, and they are authors of the Gargoylz books.

THE ILLUSTRATOR

Diane Le Feyer discovered a passion for drawing and animation at the age of five. In 2002, she graduated with honors from the Ecole Emile Cohl school of design. Diane worked as a character designer, 3D modeler, and animator in the video games industry before joining the Cartoon Saloon animation studio, where she worked as a director, animator, illustrator, and character designer. Diane was also a part of the early design and development of the movie *The Secret of Kells*.

GLOSSARY

anxiously (ANGK-shuhss-lee)—eagerly or impatiently

aurora borealis (uh-ROR-uh bor-ee-AL-iss)—colorful bands of flashing lights that sometimes can be seen at night, especially near the Artic Circle. They are also called the Northern Lights.

endangered (en-DAYN-jurd)—at risk of going extinct

fleece (FLEESS)—warm material or fabric made from a sheep's wool coat

hostile (HOSS-tuhl)—unfriendly or angry

hypothermia (hye-puh-THUR-mee-uh)—if someone is suffering from hypothermia, the person's body temperature has become dangerously low

intel (IN-tel)—information

Inupiat (uh-NOO-pee-ot)—a member of a group of Eskimos inhabiting northern Alaska. Inupiat means "the real people" in the Inupiat language.

miracle (MEER-uh-kuhl)—a remarkable or unexpected event

mission (MISH-uhn)—a special job or task

operative (OP-ur-uh-tiv)—a secret agent

trudged (TRUHJD)—walked slowly and with great effort

Polar bears live in the Arctic region. They require sea ice for hunting and breeding. They migrate each year, following the movement of the ice. While the polar bear is not endangered, their livelihood is still very much at risk from:

LOSS OF HABITAT: Global warming is the biggest threat to the polar bear. The dramatic increase in thawing Arctic sea ice has reduced the population of seals, which are the polar bear's primary source of food. Scientists predict that the sea ice may disappear completely in 20 to 30 years. That would have a catastrophic effect on the polar bear species.

OIL DRILLING: Oil is already a big business in the Arctic region. Polar bears can end up accidentally consuming chemicals from oil spills by grooming themselves or eating contaminated animals. The oil and gas industries are planning on expanding their drilling even farther into the Arctic in the near future, making the threat even greater.

PREDATORS: Polar bears have only one predator: humans. In the past, hunters were the biggest threat to the bars. Killing them is now restricted and recorded, and killings of polar bears have decreased dramatically.

BUT IT'S NOT ALL BAD FOR THE POLAR BEAR! The World Wildlife Fund strives to put a stop to climate change, which can help prevent melting sea ice. They are also working hard to prevent Arctic Sea pollution caused by shipping, fishing, and oil and gas drilling.

DISCUSSION QUESTIONS

1. Ben and Zoe name their polar bears Slurpy and Pokey. Do you have any pets? How did you pick their names? Talk about it.

2. The twins experience extremely cold weather in Alaska. Do you prefer warm or cold climates? Discuss your answers.

3. Of all the exciting things Ben and Zoe do in this book, which one would you like to do most? Why?

WRITING PROMPTS

1. Zoe and Ben use various gadgets in this book. Design your own gadget. What does it look like? What does it do? Write about your invention, and then draw a picture of it.

2. The twins get to snowboard and kayak in their polar adventure. What would you want to do if you visited Alaska? Write about your dream trip to the polar region.

3. Ben and Zoe come face to face with an angry adult polar bear. Write about your own encounter with a fierce polar bear. What would you do? How would you escape? Write about it!